Can YOU spot the aeroplane hidden in the story?

This story is for Benjamin and Caitlín who'd love to have a granny

STEPHANIE DAGG was born in Suffolk, England, but has lived in Ireland since 1992. She's married to Chris and has three children, Benjamin, Caitlín and Ruaidhrí. Stephanie is very sporty, with swimming and cycling as her favourites. She's also mad about books and computers – you can look up her website at www.booksarecool.net Stephanie's not very keen on housework and cooking. She'd much rather be writing stories! Other books by Stephanie include *Katie's Caterpillars* and *Katie's Cake*, both of which are in the popular PANDA series.

PHILLIP MORRISON has been a freelance illustrator for the last six years and is based in County Clare, in the west of Ireland. He is married, has an enormous dog called Malone and enjoys surfing. More of his illustration work can be seen at www.phillipmorrison.com

Anna's Secret Granny

Stephanie Dagg

Illustrated by Phillip Morrison

THE O'BRIEN PRESS
DUBLIN

First published 2000 by The O'Brien Press Ltd.,
20 Victoria Road, Dublin 6, Ireland.
Tel: +353 1 4923333; Fax: +353 1 4922777
E-mail: books@obrien.ie
Website: www.obrien.ie
Reprinted 2002.

ISBN: 0-86278-686-X

British Library Cataloguing-in-Publication Data
Dagg, Stephanie
Anna's secret granny. - (O'Brien flyers ; bk 5)
1.Children's stories
I.Title II.Morrison, Phillip
823.9'14[J]

2 3 4 5 6 7 8 9 10
02 03 04 05 06 07

The O'Brien Press receives
assistance from

The Arts Council
An Chomhairle Ealaíon

Editing, typesetting, layout, design: The O'Brien Press Ltd.
Illustrations: Phillip Morrison
Cover separations: C&A Print Services Ltd.
Printing: Cox & Wyman Ltd.

Chapter 1

No granny

Anna came home from school in a grumpy mood.

'What's up?' asked Mum.

'It's not **fair**,' sulked Anna. 'Melanie's granny has given her a new school bag *and* she's taking her to the circus next week. But I haven't got a granny.'

Mum sighed. 'I know. I wish you did but both your grannies died before you were born. They would **love** you so much if they were still alive.'

'Would they really?' Anna asked.

'Yes,' smiled Mum. 'I bet Granny Eileen would take you swimming every week. She was a great swimmer.

And Granny Kate would take you
to the cinema. She loved
watching films.'

'Oh, that would be **great**,'
sighed Anna.

After dinner, Anna got her crayons and a piece of paper.

She decided that if she couldn't have a **real** granny then she would draw a pretend, **secret** one.

Anna's pretend granny had a very long, thin body, and a very small head with a pointy nose. There wasn't room to give granny a right ear.

So, Anna gave her an extra big left one, and a slightly wonky smiling face!

But what exactly did grannies **look like**? Anna knew that grannies were really **old** so she gave hers grey, curly hair.

And what did they wear?

Just to be on the safe side, Anna gave her secret granny a long dress over a jumper and a pair of trousers. It looked a bit **odd**, but never mind.

Anna coloured away for ages.
At last her secret granny was finished.

Anna stuck her up on the bedroom wall.

At bedtime, Anna gave the picture a goodnight kiss. 'I wish you were **real**, Granny,' she whispered.

Chapter 2

Granny on the doorstep

Next morning, the doorbell rang.

Ring

Mum was
in the bath so
Anna ran to get it.
She looked out of
the window to see
who it was. There stood a very
weird person indeed.

It couldn't be, could it? Anna ran to look at her picture of her secret granny.

The picture was **empty**!

The person at the door was her secret granny come to **life**!

Anna flung the door open. 'Wow! Granny!' exclaimed Anna. 'You'd better come in.'

'Thank you, Anna dear!' said Granny, a bit wonkily out of her wonky mouth.

Anna and Granny stood looking at each other.

'What do I do now, dear?' asked Granny. 'I've **never** been a granny before.'

'Oh,' said Anna. 'And I've never *had* a granny before.'

She thought for a moment.

'I think grannies like cups of **tea**. Come in and I'll get you one.'

Anna and Granny went into the kitchen.

But there wasn't any tea left in the pot and Anna wasn't allowed to boil the kettle.

She couldn't ask Granny to make her own tea. That would be **rude**.

Then she had an idea. 'I know!' she smiled.

She quickly **drew** Granny a cup of tea. That should do the trick.

Granny was more than happy with her picture tea. 'That was lovely, dear! Now, what next?'

'Well, my real grannies would take me swimming or to the cinema. But I couldn't go there without asking Mum, so you'd better buy me some **treats** instead. That's something grannies do,' Anna announced.

I'd better give you some money.

So Granny set off to the shops.

Chapter 3

Granny goes shopping

Just after Granny went out the door, Mum came downstairs.

'Did I hear voices?' asked Mum.

Anna didn't know **how** to begin to tell her about Granny, so she quickly said, 'Oh, that was just me. I was playing.'

At last, Anna saw Granny coming back, and her bag was **bulging**.

'What did you get?' she squealed in excitement.

'All sorts of lovely things, dear!' smiled Granny. 'But I must say, I didn't like the shopkeepers. They looked at me in a very strange way and kept asking me if I was all right.

'Look,' said Granny, cheering up again. 'Here are your treats!'

Out of her bag she pulled a big bottle of cod liver oil, a bag of Brussels sprouts, and a huge, slimy piece of liver.

Cod liver oil

Brussel sprouts

Liver

Anna was **horrified.**

'But those aren't treats!' she wailed.

'Aren't they?' said Granny in surprise. 'They should be. I went into each shop and I asked for something that would be **good** for my granddaughter.'

Anna groaned. But then she remembered her manners so she quickly added, 'Thank you, Granny. Now, why don't you go out into the garden and I'll bring you a nice cup of tea and a slice of cake.'

Chapter 4

Mum meets Granny

Granny obediently trotted outside.

Anna was cross with Granny for
not buying her sweets so she drew her
a **horrible** bright blue piece of
cake to eat.

But Granny loved it!

Anna went back indoors to decide what to do with Granny next. Grannies were full of **surprises**. She was so busy thinking that she didn't notice Mum going out to do some gardening.

Suddenly she heard Mum shouting, 'Go away!'

'Crumbs!' yelped Anna. 'Mum's found Granny.'

She hurried outside and was just in time to see Mum **chasing** Granny across the garden.

Granny didn't reappear till bedtime.

'Sorry about Mum,' said Anna.

'Oh that's all right, dear,' smiled Granny. 'I must have given her quite a **shock**. Now, where shall I sleep? In my picture on the wall?'

'Yes,' nodded Anna.

She helped Granny climb back into her picture. She was **fascinated** to see how Granny shrunk as she stepped in.

'Goodnight, Granny,' she said holding her face up for a kiss.

Granny just smiled.

'Well, aren't you going to give me a bedtime kiss?' asked Anna. She was sure **that** was something grannies **always** did.

'Oh, yes of course, dear,' exclaimed Granny. She bent her head out of the picture and bumped Anna on the nose.

Whoops! I'm not very good at this, I'm afraid.

Then she poked her pointy nose into Anna's eye. But at last she managed to give her a **proper** kiss.

Chapter 5

Life with Granny

The next few days were tricky but fun.
Anna only **just** managed to keep
Granny a secret from Mum because
Granny kept wandering off around
the house.

Anna noticed something else about
Granny. She was **changing**.

Every day, her wonky smile got
straighter. Her pointy nose got less
pointy and her big left ear shrank. A
new ear even began to appear on the
other side of Granny's head!

She began to look like a **real**, **proper** Granny.

And Granny got much better at buying treats. Anna wrote shopping lists for her. Granny came back loaded down with sweets and comics.

But Mum caught Anna stuffing herself with sweets. She was very **cross**.

'No more sweets!' she ordered.
'Now I know why you haven't
been eating properly. You've been
spending all your pocket money
on chocolate and chews.'

So Anna had to be even more
careful to keep Granny (and her
treats) **secret**.

Anna gave Granny some treats
too. She drew her a pretty pink cottage
with a garden full of lovely flowers.
She drew a dog and a cat to keep her
company when Anna was at school.

Granny was **thrilled**.

One Thursday, Anna was very excited when Mum picked her up from school.

'I've been picked to play in the girls' football team tomorrow. You'll come to watch, won't you Mum?'

'Oh no!' groaned Mum. 'I've got a job interview tomorrow. And Daddy is away. Oh, I'm so sorry. But we **will** come to the next match, I promise.'

Anna was very upset.

Just then she remembered Granny!

'Will you come?' she begged.

But suddenly Anna's face fell. 'Oh, but everyone knows I haven't got a granny.'

'Well then,' smiled Granny, 'just tell everyone I'm your Great Aunt Matilda from Australia.'

'Brilliant!' cried Anna, clapping her hands in happiness. 'Oh Granny, it will be so **perfect** having you watching me.'

And it was!

Granny shouted and cheered loudly in a pretend Australian accent.

She jumped up and down when Anna scored the **winning goal**.

'You'll have to ask your Great
Aunt Matilda to all our matches,
Anna,' said Mrs Perks, the games
teacher. 'She really helped us play
well today!'

Anna beamed with pleasure.
It was **great** having a secret
granny!

Chapter 6

More grannies

About a month after her secret granny first appeared, Mum had a surprise for Anna. She handed her a big **package** when she came home from school.

'What is it?' asked Anna, puzzled.

'Open it and see!' laughed Mum.

Anna tore the paper off the package.

Inside were two large **photographs**.

One had 'Granny Eileen' written on it and the other had 'Granny Kate'.

'Your **grannies**,' Mum explained.

'Oh Mum,' Anna sighed. 'Thank you. They're lovely! And look, Granny Kate has got a squashy nose just like Dad!'

'And **you** have Granny Eileen's curly hair,' said Mum. 'And Granny Kate's dimples.'

'Wow, so I do!' exclaimed Anna. 'I'm just like both my grannies!'

'Can I have them in my room?' Anna asked.

'Of course,' said Mum.

Anna found the **best** place for the photographs, next to the picture of her secret granny.

Now Anna had **three** grannies in her room. She was delighted with her two real grannies. She talked to them and told them all her news.

One day she took the photos to school to show her teacher and her class.

Mum and Dad told her all
sorts of things about her grannies.

'Granny Kate, my mum, hated
spiders,' Dad said. 'I remember I
was cross with her one day so I
chased her around the house with
a huge spider! I got into terrible
trouble!'

'And my mum, that's Granny Eileen,' said Mum, 'always used to cut my hair herself but she was **hopeless**! I always had a wonky fringe. I was so embarrassed!'

Anna became so interested in her real grannies that she **forgot** all about her secret granny.

Chapter 7

Goodbye Granny

One day she came home from
school to find her secret granny
sitting on the bed, her dog
on a lead and
her cat in her arms.

'Hello, dear,' Granny said sadly.

'Hello, Granny,' replied Anna. 'Are you going somewhere?'

'Well, yes I am, dear. Do you think you could draw me a car, please?

You see, you don't really **need** me anymore, not now you have your real grannies.'

'Oh, Granny,' Anna started to cry. 'I'm sorry. I forgot all about you. It's just that there's **so much** I want to find out about my other grannies.'

'There, there,' soothed Granny. 'I've been very happy with you. But I'm not your real granny. I'm just someone you drew to buy you treats.

You see, real grannies are much, much **more** than that.

They're part of your family.
They're even part of **you**!

They love you and you love
them. You love your two real
grandmothers. I can tell by the
way you talk to them and tell
them your secrets.'

'But **where** will you go, Granny?' sniffed Anna.

'Well, now that I know what grannies do, and now that I look just like one too, I'll go and find another little boy or girl who needs a secret granny for a while,' replied Granny.

Anna got her crayons out and drew a flashy, big, red car for Granny.

She helped Granny load all her things in, and finally she helped Granny climb into the picture car.

She gave Granny a very big hug and kiss first.

'Goodbye, my special, secret granny!' she called. 'I'll **never** forget you!'

'Goodbye, my dear!' called Granny back.

Anna waved and waved until the car disappeared and the piece of paper was blank again.

Anna **sighed**. She would miss all the treats. And she would miss Granny at her football matches.

Now there were just **two** grannies in her room.

Anna looked at her photos of Granny Eileen and Granny Kate. They smiled out at her with their curls and dimples and squashy noses. Anna smiled back with her own curls and dimples, and ever so slightly squashy nose.

Anna knew they were only photos, but they were her real grannies ... and she thought that they were **perfect**.

And who knows, maybe Anna's secret granny **might** come back now and again. After all, the football team still needs 'Great Aunt Matilda'...